STEPHANIE SCOTT

BUCKLE UP

A Children's Imaginary
Journey about Self-Control

ARRIVED TO DESTINATION

YELLOW ZONE

BRAIN BREAK STATION!

SLOW DOWN

30

CAUTION

PARK NEXT EXIT

BRAIN BREAK

Dedication

THIS BOOK IS DEDICATED TO MY BRADY BUNCH of a family, including my siblings, Shawna, Ryan, Jamie, Christopher, and Tyler; my father, Dave; and my mother, Chris. In addition, A.R., thank you for reminding me to buckle up and to be patient in waiting for that rainbow after a rainy day. Thank you for helping me navigate through this thing called "life." To all of the families, children and youth, that have welcomed me into their lives throughout the years, you have been my biggest inspiration. Keep shining-always.

YES, I AM A BIRD. I AM GOING TO BE flying right beside you to guide you through a little road trip as you take up the driver's seat. You might be thinking,

ME?
DRIVE?

But I'm only a child! We will be driving only with our imaginations, of course! We are going to use our imagination as we 'buckle up' and pretend to go on a road trip to a beautiful destination!

Now remember, stay calm and be alert at all times. Life may throw some curve balls, but together, we can conquer anything! Are you ready? Breathe in calmness and breathe out any fears or worries you may have. I am right here to help.

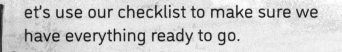

et's use our checklist to make sure we have everything ready to go.

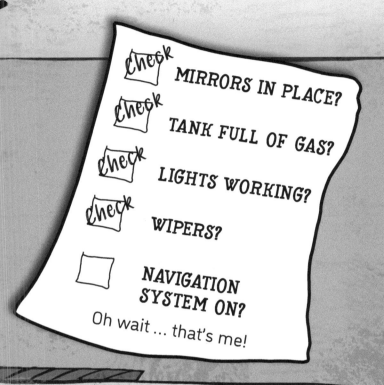

Alright, take a spot in the driver's seat and buckle up! Sometimes life has some bumpy roads, and at other times, life has a nice route with a lot of pretty scenery. Let's navigate through these roads together, keeping in mind that you always have control of the steering wheel.

It's time to back out of the driveway. Make sure you take a deep breath, and be aware of your surroundings before you back up. Being prepared is always important. Use your mirrors. Be sure to use the signal lights to communicate your plan to others.

NOW,
LET'S GET ON THE ROAD.

I t looks like there are some speed bumps ahead. You may feel nervous or a little frustrated with the bumps on the road. But you can handle them.

Just make sure you proceed with caution! Remind yourself,

"WE WILL GET THERE WHEN WE GET THERE, BUT SAFETY COMES FIRST."

Brace yourself, as we make our way slowly over the bumps.

CAUTION

REMEMBER,

if you are feeling a little uneasy or scared,
you can always pull over to the side of the
road and take a break.

BRAIN BREAK STATION!

EEEK!

IT'S STARTING TO RAIN.

Make sure you put your wipers on, to wipe away the water so that your view is clear. Prepare yourself. Remember, "After a rainy day, a rainbow must come out to play!" There we go, the rain has stopped. Take a deep breath and let's keep going. Maybe we will find that rainbow!

There's a **LITTLE BIT OF FOG** appearing. Make sure you turn on some fog lights, so you can see more clearly. Great job! We made it through.

Here comes a bit of a winding road. Make sure both hands are on the steering wheel, and your eyes are focused. Take three deep breaths to relax your hands and feet. Make sure your hands are gripping the steering wheel comfortably. Great focus!

AAAAHH,

FINALLY

a nice smooth road. Take in this moment, be aware of your surroundings, and be proud of yourself for getting this far.

UH OH! STOP!

There's a **DUCK CROSSING** the road ahead.
Sometimes waiting can be a bit annoying. Use this
time to think green thoughts as we wait our turn.
Green thoughts are helpful and positive thoughts
that help us make good choices, such as

"I AM **PATIENT**.
I CAN WAIT."
Thank you for waiting!
And now, we are back on our way.

Yellow ZONE

In the distance, I see a beautiful park with a nice pond and a play area. Would you like to go? Great! Let's keep going. Don't forget to check your rear-view mirror and be mindful of the signs along the side of the road.

30

PARK NEXT EXIT

There seems to be a bit of traffic along this street. Make sure you give some personal space in between you and other vehicles. Sometimes, it can be a bit overwhelming, with all of these vehicles around you, and there may even be some honking that you hear, but remember, it is only temporary, and you will get through it.

STAY CALM.

The traffic seems to be easing up. Stay focused on your destination. Together, we will get there soon and

WHAT'S THAT NOISE?

HMMM

You're right. I think it's a train. There's a train crossing ahead! Let's make sure that we stop and give some distance between the car and the train, so that everyone is safe. It's just like giving some personal space between your car and other cars, or between yourself and other people. You may cover your ears, if it is too loud for you.

Looks like there is a little detour coming up. There are a few options we can follow. Let's stop, think, and choose what we want to do, so that

WE CAN MAKE A DECISION.

PERSONAL SPACE ZONE!

FIRST, STOP.

Calm down, and take a slow, deep breath. What are you feeling? Let's think about our options, and if there are any consequences to them. Now, let's choose the most positive and helpful option.

WAY TO GO! THE GREEN PATH IT IS!

Okay, we are getting closer. There's a bridge for us to go over to get to the other side. We see green grass, and a river flowing very calmly. We roll down our windows all the way and feel a nice breeze, with the warmth of the sun shining on our arms and face. We smell some yummy food that people are barbequing nearby.

YUM.

What other scents do you smell?

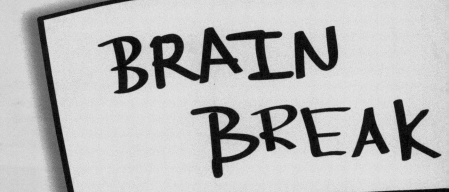

BRAIN BREAK

WE APPROACH
THE BRIDGE.

There's a stop light on the other side. It's turning yellow, so let's approach slowly. Now, the light turned red, so we need to stop and be patient.

GOOD
JOB!

After we count to twenty slowly, the light will turn green. When it does, let's go.

SLOW DOWN

HOMESTRETCH!

We are just about there. As we are pulling into the parking lot, we notice some colours in the sky.

IT'S A RAINBOW!

In fact, it's a double rainbow, for extra luck! It reminds us that there is always light at the end of the tunnel.

WE MADE IT.

You did it, with great determination! It's time to unbuckle your seatbelt, let any red, unhelpful feelings go, stretch it out, and breathe in the fun that is waiting for you! Repeat to yourself,

"I AM IN CONTROL.
I CAN NAVIGATE THROUGH ANYTHING."

OH,
BY THE WAY.

Here's a delicious popsicle for you, before you go out to play. It is quite refreshing after a long road trip, I must say. High five for getting here safely!

Have a

'TWEE TERRIFIC'
TIME!

A Message to the Readers:

IT IS UNDERSTOOD THAT KIDS CAN'T DRIVE, NOR ARE THEY encouraged to. This book brings in an imaginary journey to help children understand the concept of self-control in a creative and interactive way. Sometimes our life is like driving a car. Our bodies are like a vehicle. Every vehicle has a driver. We usually have a destination in mind. Along that journey, we may have smooth moments, and other times we may hit some bumpy roads along the way, which we have to get through. Mirrors, stoplights, and signs usually help us to regain control. They act as tools to slow us down, and help us to stop, think, and choose/create boundaries, getting us to our destination safely.

This book reminds us that sometimes we need to change our speed, slow things down, or even put the breaks on until we regain control of a situation, in better, safer, helpful, and more positive ways. It helps us to be mindful of the support team around us. It is important that you are aware of how you are feeling and look for ways to control it. Remember, your brain is very powerful. If we think positive, we will feel more positive feelings, and in turn, behave more appropriately. Driving a car takes time and practice. So does taking control of our own thoughts, feelings, and behaviours. There are various tools and techniques to use. Sometimes, it takes time to find what works and what you can add to your 'calming' toolbox.

About the Author

A GRADUATE OF RYERSON UNIVERSITY'S Child and Youth Care Program, Stephanie Scott has been involved with the care and education of vulnerable children, many of whom struggle with various emotional and intellectual challenges, for years, and has found inspiration in their various journeys. With this book, and others in the works, she hopes to provide an outlet for them to communicate their needs, gain coping tools, and learn skills and approaches that will benefit their growth and development.

When she is not working, she enjoys meditating, the outdoors, writing, and listening to music. She also loves spending time with family and friends, who bring light, love, and humour into her life, motivating her to be the best that she can be.

She currently resides in Oakville, Ontario, where she continues to pursue her goals in the child and youth care field.

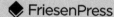

◆ FriesenPress

Suite 300 - 990 Fort St
Victoria, BC, V8V 3K2
Canada

www.friesenpress.com

ISBN
978-1-5255-4721-8 (Hardcover)
978-1-5255-4722-5 (Paperback)
978-1-5255-4723-2 (eBook)

1. JUVENILE FICTION

Distributed to the trade by The Ingram Book Company